W9-AEY-105

Dear Parents:

Congratulations! Your child is taking the first steps on an exciting journey. The destination? Independent reading!

STEP INTO READING® will help your child get there. The program offers five steps to reading success. Each step includes fun stories and colorful art or photographs. In addition to original fiction and books with favorite characters, there are Step into Reading Non-Fiction Readers, Phonics Readers and Boxed Sets, Sticker Readers, and Comic Readers—a complete literacy program with something to interest every child.

Learning to Read, Step by Step!

Ready to Read   Preschool–Kindergarten
• big type and easy words • rhyme and rhythm • picture clues
For children who know the alphabet and are eager to begin reading.

Reading with Help   Preschool–Grade 1
• basic vocabulary • short sentences • simple stories
For children who recognize familiar words and sound out new words with help.

Reading on Your Own   Grades 1–3
• engaging characters • easy-to-follow plots • popular topics
For children who are ready to read on their own.

Reading Paragraphs   Grades 2–3
• challenging vocabulary • short paragraphs • exciting stories
For newly independent readers who read simple sentences with confidence.

Ready for Chapters   Grades 2–4
• chapters • longer paragraphs • full-color art
For children who want to take the plunge into chapter books but still like colorful pictures.

STEP INTO READING® is designed to give every child a successful reading experience. The grade levels are only guides; children will progress through the steps at their own speed, developing confidence in their reading.

Remember, a lifetime love of reading starts with a single step!

Visit us on the Web!
StepIntoReading.com
randomhousekids.com

Educators and librarians, for a variety of teaching tools, visit us at RHTeachersLibrarians.com

ISBN 978-1-5247-6505-7 (trade) — ISBN 978-1-5247-6506-4 (lib. bdg.)

Printed in the United States of America   10 9 8 7 6 5 4 3 2 1

STEP INTO READING®

nickelodeon

Sing Your Song!

by Kristen L. Depken

illustrated by Nneka Myers

Random House 🏠 New York

Princess Nella
loves to sing.
Her friends Trinket,
Clod, and Garrett
love to sing, too.

They will put on
a music show.

Oh, no! An orc!

He runs to the stage.

He howls.

Everyone is scared.
Nella tries to
calm the crowd.

Nella turns into

a Princess Knight!

Her armor sparkles.

Nella uses her bow.

She shoots ribbons.

She traps the orc!

The orc is named Gork.

He is sad.

He does not want

to scare anyone.

He wants to sing!
Nella and Trinket
will teach him.

Gork tries to sing
like Trinket.

He tries to sing

like Nella.

Gork cannot sing
like Nella or Trinket.

He runs away.

Nella has an idea.
Gork cannot sing
like her friends.
But he can sing
like an orc!

Nella and her friends
look for Gork.
Uh-oh. Mud!

Nella uses her shield.
The friends ride
through the mud
to Gork's house.

Gork is still sad.
Nella tells him
that everyone has
a different voice.

Gork does not have
to sing like Nella.
Gork should just
sing like an orc!

Gork will be in the show.

He hugs his new friends.

They return
to the stage.
Gork is ready!

Nella sings.

Gork sings.

Everyone sings.

They all sound different.

They all sound
great together.
Everyone loves
the show!

Gork loves his new
friends and their
special song.